Tomie dePaola's
MOTHER
GOOSE

G·P·Putnam's Sons
New York

For all my friends in my
old hometown, Meriden, Connecticut

Wherever possible, the Mother Goose rhymes
in this book are the classic versions
collected by Peter and Iona Opie.

Illustrations copyright © 1985 by Tomie dePaola
All rights reserved. Published simultaneously in Canada.
Printed in Hong Kong by South
China Printing Co. (1988) Ltd.
Typography by Nanette Stevenson
Calligraphy by Jeanyee Wong

Library of Congress Cataloging in Publication Data
dePaola, Tomie. Tomie dePaola's Mother Goose.
Includes index.
Summary: An illustrated collection of over 200 Mother Goose nursery
rhymes, including well-known ones such as "Little Boy Blue"
and less familiar ones such as "Charlie Warlie and his cow."
1. Nursery Rhymes. 2. Children's Poetry
[1. Nursery Rhymes] I. Title. II. Title: Mother Goose.
PZ8.3.D3415Mo 1985 84-26314
ISBN 0-399-21258-2
19 20 18

Old Mother Goose,
 When she wanted to wander,
Would ride through the air
 On a very fine gander.

Mother Goose had a house,
 'Twas built in a wood,
Where an owl at the door
 For sentinel stood.

She had a son Jack,
 A plain-looking lad,
He was not very good,
 Nor yet very bad.

She sent him to market,
 A live goose he bought;
See, mother, says he,
 I have not been for nought.

Jack's goose and her gander
 Grew very fond;
They'd both eat together,
 Or swim in the pond.

Jack found one fine morning,
　　As I have been told,
His goose had laid him
　　An egg of pure gold.

Jack ran to his mother
　　The news for to tell,
She called him a good boy,
　　And said it was well.

Jack sold his gold egg
　　To a merchant untrue,
Who cheated him out of
　　A half of his due.

Then Jack went a-courting
　　A lady so gay,
As fair as the lily,
　　And sweet as the May.

The merchant and squire
　　Soon came at his back,
And began to belabour
　　The sides of poor Jack.

Then old Mother Goose
    That instant came in,
And turned her son Jack
    Into famed Harlequin.

She then with her wand
    Touched the lady so fine,
And turned her at once
    Into sweet Columbine.

The gold egg in the sea
    Was thrown away then,
When an odd fish brought her
    The egg back again.

The merchant then vowed
    The goose he would kill,
Resolving at once
    His pockets to fill.

Jack's mother came in,
    And caught the goose soon,
And mounting its back,
    Flew up to the moon.

Pussy cat, pussy cat,
    Where have you been?
I've been to London
    To look at the Queen.
Pussy cat, pussy cat,
    What did you there?
I frightened a little mouse
    Under her chair.

A diller, a dollar,
A ten o'clock scholar,
What makes you come so soon?
You used to come at ten o'clock,
But now you come at noon.

I saw a ship a-sailing,
A-sailing on the sea;
And, oh! it was all laden
With pretty things for thee!

There were comfits in the cabin,
And apples in the hold;
The sails were made of silk,
And the masts were made of gold.

The four-and-twenty sailors
That stood between the decks,
Were four-and-twenty white mice
With chains about their necks.

The captain was a duck,
With a packet on his back;
And when the ship began to move,
The captain said, "Quack! Quack!"

Lavender's blue, diddle, diddle,
　　Lavender's green;
When I am king, diddle, diddle,
　　You shall be queen.

Call up your men, diddle, diddle,
　　Set them to work,
Some to the plough, diddle, diddle,
　　Some to the cart.

Some to make hay, diddle, diddle,
　　Some to thresh corn,
Whilst you and I, diddle, diddle,
　　Keep ourselves warm.

Sing a song of sixpence,
    A pocket full of rye;
Four and twenty blackbirds,
    Baked in a pie.

When the pie was opened,
    The birds began to sing;
Was not that a dainty dish,
    To set before a king?

The king was in his counting-house,
    Counting out his money;
The queen was in the parlour
    Eating bread and honey.

The maid was in the garden,
    Hanging out the clothes,
When down came a blackbird
    And pecked off her nose.

Old woman, old woman,
    Shall we go a-shearing?
Speak a little louder, sir,
    I'm very thick of hearing.
Old woman, old woman,
    Shall I love you dearly?
Thank you very kindly, sir,
    Now I hear you clearly.

Tweedledum and Tweedledee
    Agreed to have a battle,
For Tweedledum said Tweedledee
    Had spoiled his nice new rattle.
Just then flew by a monstrous crow
    As black as a tar-barrel,
Which frightened both the heroes so,
    They quite forgot their quarrel.

Dickery, dickery, dare,
The pig flew up in the air;
The man in brown
Soon brought him down,
Dickery, dickery, dare.

Little Poll Parrot
Sat in his garret
Eating toast and tea;
A little brown mouse
Jumped into the house
And stole it all away.

When I was a little boy
    I lived by myself,
And all the bread and cheese I got
    I laid upon a shelf.

The rats and the mice
    They made such a strife,
I had to go to London town
    And get me a wife.

The streets were so broad
    And the lanes were so narrow,
I was forced to bring my wife home
    In a wheelbarrow.

The wheelbarrow broke
    And my wife had a fall,
Farewell wheelbarrow,
    Little wife and all.

Bobby Shaftoe's gone to sea,
Silver buckles at his knee;
He'll come back and marry me,
    Bonny Bobby Shaftoe.

Bobby Shaftoe's bright and fair,
Combing down his yellow hair,
He's my ain for evermair,
    Bonny Bobby Shaftoe.

Bobby Shaftoe's tall and slim,
He's always dressed so neat and trim,
The ladies they all keek at him,
    Bonny Bobby Shaftoe.

Bobby Shaftoe's getten a bairn
For to dandle in his arm;
In his arm and on his knee,
    Bobby Shaftoe loves me.

The north wind doth blow,
And we shall have snow,
And what will poor Robin do then,
    Poor thing?
He'll sit in a barn,
And keep himself warm,
And hide his head under his wing,
    Poor thing.

Rain before seven,
Fine before eleven.

Rain, rain, go away,
Come again another day,
Little Johnny wants to play.
Rain, rain, go to Spain,
Never show your face again.

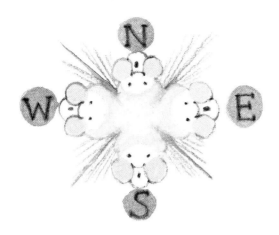

When the wind is in the east,
'Tis neither good for man nor beast;
When the wind is in the north,
The skilful fisher goes not forth;
When the wind is in the south,
It blows the bait in the fishes' mouth;
When the wind is in the west,
Then 'tis at the very best.

March winds and April showers
Bring forth May flowers.

Red sky at night,
Shepherd's delight;
Red sky in the morning,
Shepherd's warning.

If bees stay at home,
Rain will soon come;
If they fly away,
Fine will be the day.

A sunshiny shower
Won't last half an hour.

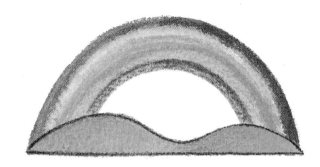

Rain on the green grass,
   And rain on the tree,
Rain on the house-top,
   But not on me.

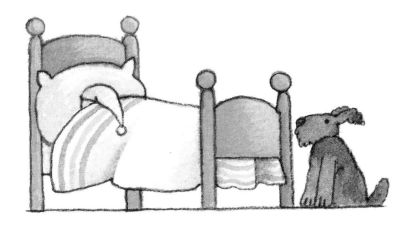

It's raining, it's pouring,
The old man's snoring;
He got into bed
And bumped his head
And couldn't get up in the morning.

Cold and raw the north wind doth blow,
Bleak in the morning early;
All the hills are covered with snow,
And winter's now come fairly.

Blow, wind, blow!
And go, mill, go!
That the miller may grind his corn;
That the baker may take it,
And into bread make it,
And bring us a loaf in the morn.

Old Mother Hubbard
Went to the cupboard,
To fetch her poor dog a bone;
But when she got there
The cupboard was bare
And so the poor dog had none.

She went to the baker's
To buy him some bread;
But when she came back
The poor dog was dead.

She went to the undertaker's
To buy him a coffin;
But when she came back
The poor dog was laughing.

She took a clean dish
To get him some tripe;
But when she came back
He was smoking a pipe.

She went to the fishmonger's
To buy him some fish;
But when she came back
He was licking the dish.

She went to the tavern
For white wine and red;
But when she came back
The dog stood on his head.

She went to the fruiterer's
To buy him some fruit;
But when she came back
He was playing the flute.

She went to the tailor's
      To buy him a coat;
But when she came back
      He was riding a goat.

She went to the hatter's
      To buy him a hat;
But when she came back
      He was feeding the cat.

She went to the barber's
      To buy him a wig;
But when she came back
      He was dancing a jig.

She went to the cobbler's
      To buy him some shoes;
But when she came back
      He was reading the news.

She went to the seamstress
      To buy him some linen;
But when she came back
      The dog was a-spinning.

She went to the hosier's
      To buy him some hose;
But when she came back
      He was dressed in his clothes.

The dame made a curtsey,
      The dog made a bow;
The dame said, Your Servant,
      The dog said, Bow-bow.

23

There was a crooked man,
    And he walked a crooked mile,
He found a crooked sixpence
    Against a crooked stile;
He bought a crooked cat,
    Which caught a crooked mouse,
And they all lived together
    In a little crooked house.

Little Boy Blue,
    Come blow your horn,
The sheep's in the meadow,
    The cow's in the corn.
Where is the boy
    Who looks after the sheep?
He's under a haystack,
    Fast asleep.
Will you wake him?
    No, not I,
For if I do,
    He's sure to cry.

There came an old woman from
        France
Who taught grown-up children to
        dance;
    But they were so stiff,
    She sent them home in a sniff,
This sprightly old woman from
        France.

Three wise men of Gotham
Went to sea in a bowl
If the bowl had been stronger,
My story would have been longer.

Ride a cock-horse to Banbury Cross,
To see a fine lady upon a white horse;
Rings on her fingers and bells on her toes,
And she shall have music wherever she goes.

Taffy was a Welshman,
    Taffy was a thief,
Taffy came to my house
    And stole a piece of beef.

I went to Taffy's house,
    Taffy wasn't in,
I jumped upon his Sunday hat
    And poked it with a pin.

Taffy was a Welshman,
    Taffy was a sham,
Taffy came to my house
    And stole a leg of lamb.

I went to Taffy's house,
    Taffy was not there,
I hung his coat and trousers
    To roast before a fire.

Taffy was a Welshman,
    Taffy was a cheat,
Taffy came to my house
    And stole a piece of meat.

I went to Taffy's house,
    Taffy wasn't home;
Taffy came to my house
    And stole a marrow bone.

Ladies and gentlemen come to
    supper—
Hot boiled beans and very good
    butter.

Hush, baby, my dolly, I pray you
    don't cry,
And I'll give you some bread, and
    some milk by-and-by;
Or perhaps you like custard, or,
    maybe a tart,
Then to either you're welcome, with
    all my heart.

Molly, my sister, and I fell out,
And what do you think it was all about?
She loved coffee and I loved tea,
And that was the reason we couldn't agree.

Jack Sprat could eat no fat,
    His wife could eat no lean,
And so between them both, you see,
    They licked the platter clean.

Little Tommy Tucker
    Sings for his supper:
What shall we give him?
    White bread and butter.
How shall he cut it
    Without e'er a knife?
How will he be married
    Without e'er a wife?

Polly put the kettle on,
Polly put the kettle on,
Polly put the kettle on,
    We'll all have tea.

Sukey take it off again,
Sukey take it off again,
Sukey take it off again,
    They've all gone away.

Simple Simon met a pieman
    Going to the fair;
Says Simple Simon to the pieman,
    Let me taste your ware.

Says the pieman to Simple Simon,
    Show me first your penny;
Says Simple Simon to the pieman,
    Indeed I have not any.

Simple Simon went a-fishing,
    For to catch a whale;
All the water he had got
    Was in his mother's pail.

He went to catch a dickey bird,
    And thought he could not fail,
Because he'd got a little salt,
    To put upon its tail.

Once Simon made a great snowball,
    And brought it in to roast;
He laid it down before the fire,
    And soon the ball was lost.

He went for water in a sieve,
    But soon it all ran through;
And now poor Simple Simon
    Bids you all adieu.

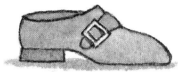

1, 2,
Buckle my shoe;

3, 4,
Knock at the door;

5, 6,
Pick up sticks;

7, 8,
Lay them straight;

9, 10,
A big fat hen;

11, 12,
Dig and delve;

13, 14,
Maids a-courting;

15, 16,
Maids in the kitchen;

17, 18,
Maids in waiting;

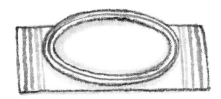

19, 20,
My plate's empty.

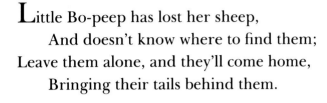

Little Bo-peep has lost her sheep,
    And doesn't know where to find them;
Leave them alone, and they'll come home,
    Bringing their tails behind them.

Little Bo-peep fell fast asleep,
    And dreamt she heard them bleating;
But when she awoke, she found it a joke,
    For they were still a-fleeting.

Then up she took her little crook,
    Determined for to find them;
She found them indeed, but it made her heart bleed
    For they'd left their tails behind them.

It happened one day, as Bo-peep did stray
    Into a meadow hard by,
There she espied their tails side by side,
    All hung on a tree to dry.

She heaved a sigh, and wiped her eye,
    And over the hillocks went rambling,
And tried what she could, as a shepherdess should,
    To tack again each to its lambkin.

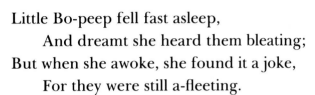

High diddle doubt, my candle's out
My little maid is not at home;
Saddle my hog and bridle my dog,
And fetch my little maid home.

Dance, little Baby, dance up high!
Never mind, Baby, Mother is by.
Crow and caper, caper and crow,
There, little Baby, there you go!
Up to the ceiling, down to the
    ground,
Backwards and forwards, round
    and round;
Dance, little Baby and Mother
    will sing,
With the merry coral, ding, ding,
    ding!

"I went up one pair of stairs."
   "Just like me."
"I went up two pairs of stairs."
   "Just like me."
"I went into a room."
   "Just like me."
"I looked out of a window."
   "Just like me."
"And there I saw a monkey."
   "Just like me."

To make your candles last for aye,
You wives and maids give ear-O!
To put them out's the only way,
Says honest John Boldero.

Jerry Hall,
He is so small,
A rat could eat him,
Hat and all.

Little girl, little girl,
　　Where have you been?
I've been to see grandmother
　　Over the green.
What did she give you?
　　Milk in a can.
What did you say for it?
　　Thank you, Grandam.

What are little boys made of, made of?
What are little boys made of?
　　Frogs and snails
　　And puppy-dogs' tails,
That's what little boys are made of.

What are little girls made of, made of?
What are little girls made of?
　　Sugar and spice
　　And all things nice,
That's what little girls are made of.

Old King Cole
Was a merry old soul,
And a merry old soul was he;
He called for his pipe,
And he called for his bowl,
And he called for his fiddlers three.

Every fiddler he had a fiddle,
And a very fine fiddle had he;
Oh, there's none so rare
As can compare
With King Cole and his fiddlers three.

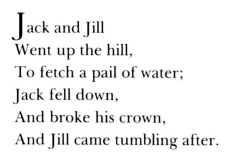

Jack and Jill
Went up the hill,
To fetch a pail of water;
Jack fell down,
And broke his crown,
And Jill came tumbling after.

Then up Jack got,
And home did trot,
As fast as he could caper;
To old Dame Dob,
Who patched his nob
With vinegar and brown paper.

When Jill came in,
How she did grin
To see Jack's paper plaster;
Her mother, vexed,
Did whip her next,
For laughing at Jack's disaster.

Now Jack did laugh
And Jill did cry,
But her tears did soon abate;
Then Jill did say,
That they should play
At see-saw across the gate.

Goosey, goosey gander,
    Whither shall I wander?
Upstairs and downstairs
    And in my lady's chamber.
There I met an old man
    Who would not say his prayers,
I took him by the left leg
    And threw him down the stairs.

Hickety, pickety, my black hen,
She lays eggs for gentlemen;
Gentlemen come every day
To see what my black hen doth lay.

Cock a doodle doo!
My dame has lost her shoe,
My master's lost his fiddling stick
And knows not what to do.

Cock a doodle doo!
What is my dame to do?
Till master finds his fiddling stick
She'll dance without her shoe.

Cock a doodle doo!
My dame has found her shoe,
And master's found his fiddling stick,
Sing doodle doodle doo.

Cock a doodle doo!
My dame will dance with you,
While master fiddles his fiddling stick
For dame and doodle doo.

Barber, barber, shave a pig,
How many hairs will make a wig?
Four and twenty, that's enough.
Give the barber a pinch of snuff.

Bow, wow, wow,
Whose dog art thou?
Little Tom Tinker's dog,
Bow, wow, wow.

The lion and the unicorn
　　Were fighting for the crown;
The lion beat the unicorn
　　All around the town.

Some gave them white bread,
　　And some gave them brown;
Some gave them plum cake
　　And drummed them out of town.

I had a cat and the cat pleased me,
I fed my cat by yonder tree;
    Cat goes fiddle-i-fee.

I had a hen and the hen pleased me,
I fed my hen by yonder tree;
    Hen goes chimmy-chuck, chimmy-chuck,
    Cat goes fiddle-i-fee.

I had a duck and the duck pleased me,
I fed my duck by yonder tree;
    Duck goes quack, quack,
    Hen goes chimmy-chuck, chimmy-chuck,
    Cat goes fiddle-i-fee.

I had a goose and the goose pleased me,
I fed my goose by yonder tree;
    Goose goes swishy, swashy,
    Duck goes quack, quack,
    Hen goes chimmy-chuck, chimmy-chuck,
    Cat goes fiddle-i-fee.

I had a sheep and the sheep pleased me,
I fed my sheep by yonder tree;
  Sheep goes baa, baa,
  Goose goes swishy, swashy,
  Duck goes quack, quack,
  Hen goes chimmy-chuck, chimmy-chuck,
  Cat goes fiddle-i-fee.

I had a pig and the pig pleased me,
I fed my pig by yonder tree;
  Pig goes griffy, gruffy,
  Sheep goes baa, baa,
  Goose goes swishy, swashy,
  Duck goes quack, quack,
  Hen goes chimmy-chuck, chimmy-chuck,
  Cat goes fiddle-i-fee.

I had a cow and the cow pleased me,
I fed my cow by yonder tree;
  Cow goes moo, moo,
  Pig goes griffy, gruffy,
  Sheep goes baa, baa,
  Goose goes swishy, swashy,
  Duck goes quack, quack,
  Hen goes chimmy-chuck, chimmy-chuck,
  Cat goes fiddle-i-fee.

I had a horse and the horse pleased me,
I fed my horse by yonder tree;
    Horse goes neigh, neigh,
    Cow goes moo, moo,
    Pig goes griffy, gruffy,
    Sheep goes baa, baa,
    Goose goes swishy, swashy,
    Duck goes quack, quack,
    Hen goes chimmy-chuck, chimmy-chuck,
    Cat goes fiddle-i-fee.

I had a dog and the dog pleased me,
I fed my dog by yonder tree;
    Dog goes bow-wow, bow-wow,
    Horse goes neigh, neigh,
    Cow goes moo, moo,
    Pig goes griffy, gruffy,
    Sheep goes baa, baa,
    Goose goes swishy, swashy,
    Duck goes quack, quack,
    Hen goes chimmy-chuck, chimmy-chuck,
    Cat goes fiddle-i-fee.

Charlie Warlie had a cow,
Black and white about the brow;
Open the gate and let her through,
Charlie Warlie's old cow.

Oh where, oh where has my little dog gone?
　Oh where, oh where can he be?
With his ears cut short and his tail cut long,
　Oh where, oh where is he?

This little pig went to market,
This little pig stayed at home,
This little pig had roast beef,
This little pig had none,
And this little pig cried, Wee-wee-
　　wee-wee-wee,
I can't find my way home.

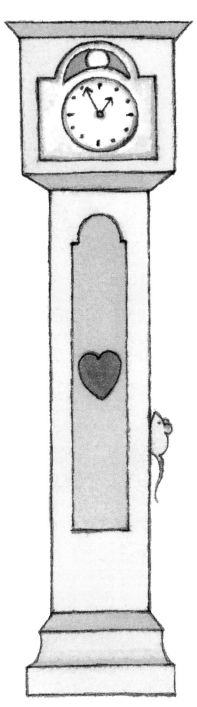

Hickory, dickory, dock,
The mouse ran up the clock.
The clock struck one,
The mouse ran down,
Hickory, dickory, dock.

There was a rat, for want of stairs,
Went down a rope to say his prayers.

There were once two cats of Kilkenny.
Each thought there was one cat too many;
So they fought and they fit,
And they scratched and they bit,
Till, excepting their nails,
And the tips of their tails,
Instead of two cats, there weren't any.

A wise old owl sat in an oak,
The more he heard the less he spoke;
The less he spoke the more he heard.
Why aren't we all like that wise old bird?

I had a little hen,
    The prettiest ever seen;
She washed up the dishes,
    And kept the house clean.
She went to the mill
    To fetch me some flour,
And always got home
    In less than an hour.
She baked me my bread,
    She brewed me my ale,
She sat by the fire
    And told a fine tale.

Hey diddle, diddle,
The cat and the fiddle,
The cow jumped over the moon;
The little dog laughed
To see such sport,
And the dish ran away with the spoon.

Baa, baa, black sheep,
  Have you any wool?
Yes, sir, yes, sir,
  Three bags full;
One for the master,
  And one for the dame,
And one for the little boy
  Who lives down the lane.

The cock's on the roof top
  Blowing his horn,
The bull's in the barn
  A-threshing the corn,
The maids in the meadow
  Are making the hay,
The ducks in the river
  Are swimming away.

Three little kittens
They lost their mittens,
    And they began to cry,
Oh, Mother dear,
We sadly fear
    Our mittens we have lost.
What! lost your mittens,
You naughty kittens!
    Then you shall have no pie.
    Mee-ow, mee-ow, mee-ow.
    No, you shall have no pie.

The three little kittens
They found their mittens,
    And they began to cry,
Oh, Mother dear,
See here, see here,
    Our mittens we have found.
Put on your mittens,
You silly kittens,
    And you shall have some pie.
    Purr-r, purr-r, purr-r,
    Oh, let us have some pie.

The three little kittens
Put on their mittens
    And soon ate up the pie;
Oh, Mother dear,
We greatly fear
    Our mittens we have soiled.
What! soiled your mittens,
You naughty kittens!
    Then they began to sigh,
    Mee-ow, mee-ow, mee-ow,
    Then they began to sigh.

The three little kittens
They washed their mittens,
    And hung them out to dry;
Oh, Mother dear,
Do you not hear,
    Our mittens we have washed.
What! washed your mittens,
Then you're good kittens,
    But I smell a rat close by.
    Mee-ow, mee-ow, mee-ow,
    We smell a rat close by.

Hector Protector was dressed all in green;
Hector Protector was sent to the Queen.
The Queen did not like him,
No more did the King;
So Hector Protector was sent back again.

Here am I,
      Little Jumping Joan;
When nobody's with me
      I'm all alone.

Jack be nimble,
      Jack be quick,
Jack jump over
      The candlestick.

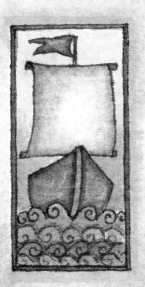

Dance to your daddy,
   My little babby,
Dance to your daddy,
   My little lamb.

You shall have a fishy
   In a little dishy,
You shall have a fishy
   When the boat comes in.

You shall have an apple,
   You shall have a plum,
You shall have a rattle-basket
   When your daddy comes home.

Mother, may I go out to swim?
Yes, my darling daughter.
Hang your clothes on a hickory limb
And don't go near the water.

There was an old woman
Lived under a hill,
And if she's not gone
She lives there still.

Dingty diddlety,
My mammy's maid,
She stole oranges,
I am afraid;
Some in her pocket,
Some in her sleeve,
She stole oranges,
I do believe.

Rub-a-dub-dub,
Three men in a tub,
And how do you think they got there?
The butcher, the baker,
The candlestick-maker,
They all jumped out of a rotten
    potato,
'Twas enough to make a man stare.

Diddle, diddle, dumpling, my son John,
Went to bed with his trousers on;
One shoe off, and one shoe on,
Diddle, diddle, dumpling, my son John.

Georgie Porgie, pudding and pie,
Kissed the girls and made them cry;
When the boys came out to play,
Georgie Porgie ran away.

Little Miss Muffet
Sat on a tuffet,
Eating her curds and whey;
There came a big spider,
Who sat down beside her
And frightened Miss Muffet away.

Peter, Peter, pumpkin eater,
Had a wife and couldn't keep her;
He put her in a pumpkin shell
And there he kept her very well.

Tom, Tom, the piper's son,
Stole a pig and away he run;
    The pig was eat,
    And Tom was beat,
And Tom went howling down the street.

Oh, soldier, soldier, will you marry me,
 With your musket, fife, and drum?
Oh no, pretty maid, I cannot marry you,
 For I have no coat to put on.

Then away she went to the tailor's shop
 As fast as legs could run,
And bought him one of the very very best,
 And the soldier put it on.

Oh, soldier, soldier, will you marry me,
 With your musket, fife, and drum?
Oh no, pretty maid, I cannot marry you,
 For I have no shoes to put on.

Then away she went to the cobbler's shop
    As fast as legs could run,
And bought him a pair of the very very best,
    And the soldier put them on.

Oh, soldier, soldier, will you marry me,
    With your musket, fife, and drum?
Oh no, pretty maid, I cannot marry you,
    For I have no hat to put on.

Then away she went to the hatter's shop
    As fast as legs could run,
And bought him one of the very very best,
    And the soldier put it on.

Oh, soldier, soldier, will you marry me,
    With your musket, fife, and drum?
Oh no, pretty maid, I cannot marry you,
    For I have a wife at home.

61

Humpty Dumpty sat on a wall,
Humpty Dumpty had a great fall;
All the King's horses and all the King's men
Couldn't put Humpty together again.

Mary, Mary, quite contrary,
    How does your garden grow?
With silver bells and cockle shells,
    And pretty maids all in a row.

There was an old woman who lived in a shoe,
She had so many children she didn't know what to do;
She gave them some broth without any bread;
She whipped them all soundly and put them to bed.

See-saw, Margery Daw,
Jacky shall have a new master;
Jacky shall have but a penny a day,
Because he can't work any faster.

Come, butter, come,
Come, butter, come;
Peter stands at the gate
Waiting for a butter cake.
Come, butter, come.

Knock on the door,
Peek in.
Lift up the latch,
And walk in.

Pat-a-cake, pat-a-cake, baker's man,
Bake me a cake as fast as you can;
Pat it and prick it, and mark it with T,
Put it in the oven for Tommy and me.

Bye, baby bunting,
Daddy's gone a-hunting,
Gone to get a rabbit skin
To wrap the baby bunting in.

Hush, little baby, don't say a word,
Papa's going to buy you a mocking bird.

If the mocking bird won't sing,
Papa's going to buy you a diamond ring.

If the diamond ring turns to brass,
Papa's going to buy you a looking-glass.

If the looking-glass gets broke,
Papa's going to buy you a billy-goat.

If that billy-goat runs away,
Papa's going to buy you another today.

MONDAY

TUESDAY

WEDNESDAY

THURSDAY

Monday's child is fair of face,
Tuesday's child is full of grace,
Wednesday's child is full of woe,
Thursday's child has far to go,
Friday's child is loving and giving,
Saturday's child works hard for its living,
But the child that's born on the Sabbath day
Is bonny and blithe, and good and gay.

FRIDAY

SATURDAY

SUNDAY

Good morrow to you, Valentine.
Curl your locks as I do mine,
Two before and three behind.
Good morrow to you, Valentine.

The rose is red, the violet's blue,
The honey's sweet, and so are you.
Thou art my love and I am thine;
I drew thee to my Valentine.
The lot was cast and then I drew,
And fortune said it should be you.

One I love,
Two I love,
Three I love, I say,
Four I love with all my heart,
Five I cast away;
Six he loves me,
Seven he don't,
Eight we're lovers both;
Nine he comes,
Ten he tarries,
Eleven he courts,
Twelve he marries.

Roses are red,
    Violets are blue,
Sugar is sweet
    And so are you.

He loves me,
    He don't,
He'll have me,
    He won't,
He would
    If he could,
But he can't
    So he don't.

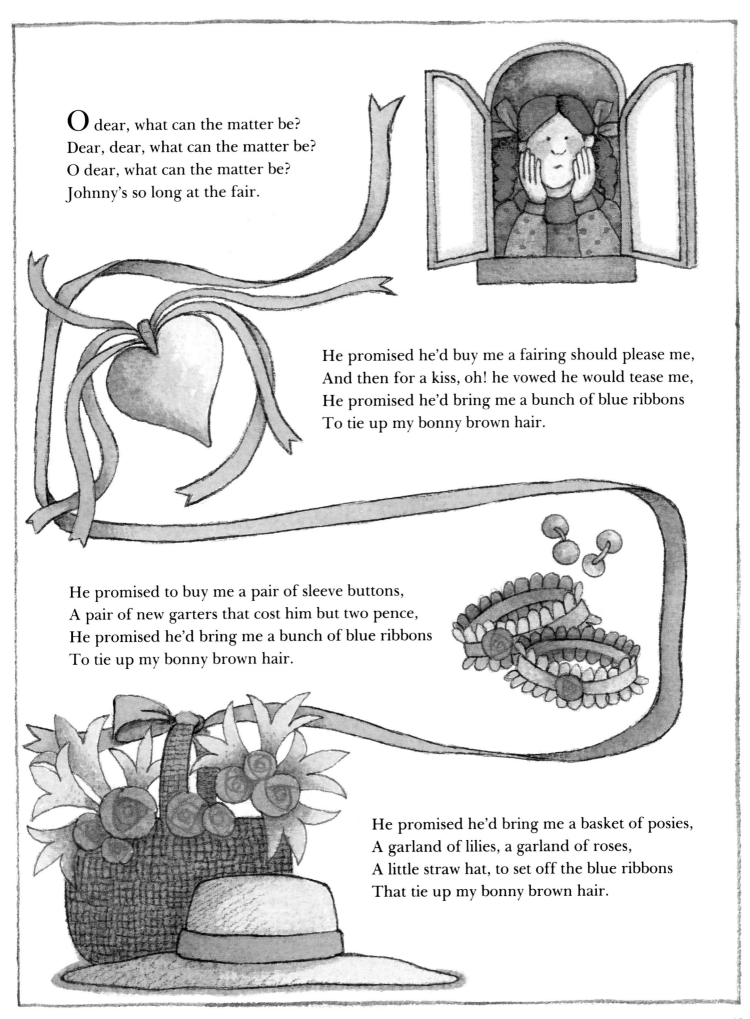

O dear, what can the matter be?
Dear, dear, what can the matter be?
O dear, what can the matter be?
Johnny's so long at the fair.

He promised he'd buy me a fairing should please me,
And then for a kiss, oh! he vowed he would tease me,
He promised he'd bring me a bunch of blue ribbons
To tie up my bonny brown hair.

He promised to buy me a pair of sleeve buttons,
A pair of new garters that cost him but two pence,
He promised he'd bring me a bunch of blue ribbons
To tie up my bonny brown hair.

He promised he'd bring me a basket of posies,
A garland of lilies, a garland of roses,
A little straw hat, to set off the blue ribbons
That tie up my bonny brown hair.

Hot cross buns, hot cross buns;
One a penny poker,
Two a penny tongs,
Three a penny fire shovel,
Hot cross buns.

Curly locks, Curly locks,
    Wilt thou be mine?
Thou shalt not wash dishes
    Nor yet feed the swine;
But sit on a cushion
    And sew a fine seam,
And feed upon strawberries,
    Sugar and cream.

Six little mice sat down to spin;
Pussy passed by and she peeped in.
What are you doing, my little men?
Weaving coats for gentlemen.
Shall I come in and cut off your threads?
No, no, Mistress Pussy, you'd bite off our heads.
Oh, no, I'll not; I'll help you to spin.
That may be so, but you don't come in.

Three blind mice, see how they run!
They all ran after the farmer's wife,
Who cut off their tails with a carving knife,
Did you ever see such a thing in your life,
    As three blind mice?

Great A, little a,
    Bouncing B,
The cat's in the cupboard
    And can't see me.

Ladybird, ladybird,
    Fly away home,
Your house is on fire
    And your children all gone;
All except one
    And that's little Ann
And she has crept under
    The warming pan.

Ring-a-ring o'roses,
A pocket full of posies,
   A-tishoo! A-tishoo!
We all fall down.

The cows are in the meadow
Lying fast asleep,
   A-tishoo! A-tishoo!
We all get up again.

There was an old woman tossed up in a basket,
   Seventeen times as high as the moon;
Where she was going I couldn't but ask it,
   For in her hand she carried a broom.

Old woman, old woman, old woman, quoth I,
   Where are you going to up so high?
To brush the cobwebs off the sky!
   May I go with you? Aye, by-and-by.

The man in the moon
Came down too soon,
And asked his way to Norwich;
He went by the south,
And burnt his mouth
With supping cold plum porridge.

One misty, moisty morning,
    When cloudy was the weather,
I met a little old man
    Clothed all in leather.

He began to compliment,
    And I began to grin,
How do you do, and how do you do,
    And how do you do again?

Here we go round the mulberry bush,
The mulberry bush, the mulberry bush,
Here we go round the mulberry bush,
On a cold and frosty morning.

This is the way we wash our hands,
Wash our hands, wash our hands,
This is the way we wash our hands,
On a cold and frosty morning.

This is the way we wash our clothes,
Wash our clothes, wash our clothes,
This is the way we wash our clothes,
On a cold and frosty morning.

This is the way we go to school,
Go to school, go to school,
This is the way we go to school,
On a cold and frosty morning.

This is the way we come out of school,
Come out of school, come out of school,
This is the way we come out of school,
On a cold and frosty morning.

There was a little girl, and she had a little curl
Right in the middle of her forehead;
When she was good she was very very good,
But when she was bad she was horrid.

Cobbler, cobbler, mend my shoe,
Get it done by half past two;
Stitch it up, and stitch it down,
Then I'll give you half a crown.

Cross-patch,
Draw the latch,
Sit by the fire and spin;
Take a cup,
And drink it up,
Then call your neighbours in.

Thirty days hath September,
April, June, and November;
All the rest have thirty-one,
Excepting February alone,
And that has twenty-eight days clear
And twenty-nine in each leap year.

Daffy-down-dilly is new come to town,
With a yellow petticoat, and a green gown.

I had a little nut tree,
    Nothing would it bear
But a silver nutmeg
    And a golden pear;
The king of Spain's daughter
    Came to visit me,
And all for the sake
    Of my little nut tree.

Doctor Foster went to Gloucester
In a shower of rain;
He stepped in a puddle,
Right up to his middle,
And never went there again.

As I was going to St. Ives,
I met a man with seven wives;
Each wife had seven sacks,
Each sack had seven cats,
Each cat had seven kits:
Kits, cats, sacks, and wives,
How many were there going to St. Ives?
(One or None)

Yankee Doodle came to town,
Riding on a pony;
He stuck a feather in his cap
And called it macaroni.

Hark, hark,
The dogs do bark,
The beggars are coming to town;
Some in rags,
And some in jags,
And one in a velvet gown.

I had a dog
    Whose name was Buff;
I sent him for
    A bag of snuff;
He broke the bag
    And spilt the stuff,
And that was all
    My penny's worth.

I love little pussy,
    Her coat is so warm,
And if I don't hurt her
    She'll do me no harm.
So I'll not pull her tail,
    Nor drive her away,
But pussy and I
    Very gently will play.
She shall sit by my side,
    And I'll give her some food;
And pussy will love me
    Because I am good.

Dame Trot and her cat
    Sat down for a chat;
The Dame sat on this side
    And puss sat on that.

Puss, says the Dame,
    Can you catch a rat,
Or a mouse in the dark?
    Purr, says the cat.

I had a little pony,
    His name was Dapple Gray;
I lent him to a lady
    To ride a mile away.
She whipped him, she slashed him,
    She rode him through the mire;
I would not lend my pony now,
    For all the lady's hire.

St. Dunstan, as the story goes,
Once pulled the devil by his nose,
With red hot tongs, which made him roar,
That could be heard ten miles or more.

Little King Pippin
    He built a fine hall,
Pie-crust and pastry-crust
    That was the wall;
The windows were made
    Of black pudding and white,
And slated with pancakes,
    You ne'er saw the like.

The Queen of Hearts
She made some tarts,
All on a summer's day;
The Knave of Hearts
He stole those tarts,
And took them clean away.

The King of Hearts
Called for the tarts,
And beat the knave full sore;
The Knave of Hearts
Brought back the tarts,
And vowed he'd steal no more.

Lucy Locket lost her pocket,
　Kitty Fisher found it;
Not a penny was there in it,
　Only ribbon round it.

I do not like thee, Doctor Fell,
The reason why I cannot tell;
But I know, and know full well,
I do not like thee, Doctor Fell.

Elsie Marley is grown so fine,
She won't get up to feed the swine,
But lies in bed till eight or nine.
　Lazy Elsie Marley.

Terence McDiddler,
　　The three-stringed fiddler,
Can charm, if you please,
　　The fish from the seas.

Little Betty Blue
　　Lost her holiday shoe,
What can little Betty do?
　　Give her another
　　To match the other,
And then she may walk out in two.

Tommy Trot, a man of law,
Sold his bed and lay upon straw;
Sold the straw and slept on grass,
To buy his wife a looking-glass.

Little Tommy Tittlemouse
Lived in a little house;
He caught fishes
In other men's ditches.

Little Polly Flinders
Sat among the cinders,
Warming her pretty little toes;
Her mother came and caught her,
And whipped her little daughter
For spoiling her nice new clothes.

Gregory Griggs, Gregory Griggs,
Had twenty-seven different wigs.
He wore them up, he wore them down,
To please the people of the town;
He wore them east, he wore them west,
But he never could tell which he loved the best.

Charley Barley, butter and eggs,
Sold his wife for three duck eggs.
When the ducks began to lay
Charley Barley flew away.

Anna Maria she sat on the fire;
The fire was too hot, she sat on the pot;
The pot was too round, she sat on the ground;
The ground was too flat, she sat on the cat;
The cat ran away with Maria on her back.

As Tommy Snooks and Bessy Brooks
Were walking out one Sunday,
Says Tommy Snooks to Bessy Brooks,
Tomorrow will be Monday.

My mother said
That I never should
Play with the gipsies
In the wood;
If I did she would say,
Naughty girl to disobey,
Your hair shan't curl,
Your shoes shan't shine,
You naughty girl
You shan't be mine.
My father said
That if I did
He'd bang my head
With the teapot lid.

The wood was dark
The grass was green,
Up comes Sally
With a tambourine;
Alpaca frock,
New scarf-shawl,
White straw bonnet
And a pink parasol.
I went to the river—
No ship to get across,
I paid ten shillings
For an old blind horse;
I up on his back
And off in a crack,
Sally tell my mother
I shall never come back.

Willy boy, Willy boy, where are you going?
I will go with you if that I may.
I'm going to the meadow to see them a-mowing,
I am going to help them to make the new hay.

My maid Mary,
    She minds the dairy,
While I go a-hoeing and mowing each morn;
    Merrily run the reel,
    And the little spinning wheel,
Whilst I am singing and mowing my corn.

There was a little boy went into a barn,
And lay down on some hay;
An owl came out and flew about,
And the little boy ran away.

The boughs do shake and the bells do ring,
So merrily comes our harvest in,
Our harvest in, our harvest in,
So merrily comes our harvest in.

We've ploughed, we've sowed,
We've reaped, we've mowed,
We've got our harvest in.

Puss came dancing out of a barn
With a pair of bagpipes under her arm;
She could sing nothing, but, Fiddle cum fee,
The mouse has married the humble-bee.
Pipe, cat—dance, mouse—
We'll have a wedding at our good house.

First in a carriage,
	Second in a gig,
Third on a donkey,
	And fourth on a pig.

Pussy cat Mole jumped over a coal
And in her best petticoat burnt a great hole.
Poor pussy's weeping, she'll have no more milk
Until her best petticoat's mended with silk.

Three young rats with black felt hats,
Three young ducks with white straw flats,
Three young dogs with curling tails,
Three young cats with demi-veils,
Went out to walk with two young pigs
In satin vests and sorrel wigs;
But suddenly it chanced to rain
And so they all went home again.

Chook, chook, chook, chook, chook,
    Good morning, Mrs. Hen.
How many chickens have you got?
    Madam, I've got ten.
Four of them are yellow,
    And four of them are brown,
And two of them are speckled red,
    The nicest in the town.

To market, to market,
    To buy a plum bun;
Home again, home again,
    Market is done.

As I was going to Banbury,
    Upon a summer's day,
My dame had butter, eggs, and fruit,
    And I had corn and hay.
Joe drove the ox, and Tom the swine,
    Dick took the foal and mare;
I sold them all—then home to dine,
    From famous Banbury fair.

This is the way the ladies ride,
    Nim, nim, nim, nim.
This is the way the gentlemen ride,
    Trim, trim, trim, trim.
This is the way the farmers ride,
    Trot, trot, trot, trot.
This is the way the huntsmen ride,
    A-gallop, a-gallop, a-gallop, a-gallop.
This is the way the ploughboys ride,
    Hobble-dy-gee, hobble-dy-gee.

The winds they did blow,
  The leaves they did wag;
Along came a beggar boy,
  And put me in his bag.

He took me up to London,
  A lady did me buy,
Put me in a silver cage,
  And hung me up on high.

With apples by the fire,
  And nuts for to crack,
Besides a little feather bed
  To rest my little back.

On the first of March,
The crows begin to search;
By the first of April
They are sitting still;
By the first of May
They've all flown away,
Coming greedy back again
With October's wind and rain.

Mr. East gave a feast;
Mr. North laid the cloth;
Mr. West did his best;
Mr. South burnt his mouth
With eating a cold potato.

Brave news is come to town,
    Brave news is carried;
Brave news is come to town,
    Jemmy Dawson's married.

First he got a porridge-pot,
    Then he bought a ladle;
Then he got a wife and child,
    And then he bought a cradle.

When Jacky's a good boy,
    He shall have cakes and custard;
But when he does nothing but cry,
    He shall have nothing but mustard.

Little Jack Horner
Sat in the corner,
Eating his Christmas pie;
He put in his thumb,
And pulled out a plum,
And said, What a good boy am I!

Hoddley, poddley, puddle and fogs,
Cats are to marry the poodle dogs;
Cats in blue jackets and dogs in red hats,
What will become of the mice and the rats?

I love sixpence, jolly little sixpence,
  I love sixpence better than my life;
I spent a penny of it, I lent a penny of it,
  And I took fourpence home to my wife.

Oh, my little fourpence, jolly little fourpence,
  I love fourpence better than my life;
I spent a penny of it, I lent a penny of it,
  And I took twopence home to my wife.

Oh, my little twopence, jolly little twopence,
  I love twopence better than my life;
I spent a penny of it, I lent a penny of it,
  And I took nothing home to my wife.

Oh, my little nothing, jolly little nothing,
  What will nothing buy for my wife?
I have nothing, I spend nothing,
  I love nothing better than my wife.

Little Tee-wee,
He went to sea,
In an open boat;
And when it was afloat,
The little boat bended,
My story's ended.

One, two, three, four, five,
Once I caught a fish alive,
Six, seven, eight, nine, ten,
Then I let it go again.
Why did you let it go?
Because it bit my finger so.
Which finger did it bite?
The little finger on the right.

Ickle ockle, blue bockle,
Fishes in the sea,
If you want a pretty maid,
Please choose me.

I went up the high hill,
There I saw a climbing goat;
I went down by the running rill,
There I saw a ragged sheep;
I went out to the roaring sea,
There I saw a tossing boat;
I went under the green tree,
There I saw two doves asleep.

There was a little woman,
    As I have heard tell,
She went to market
    Her eggs for to sell,
She went to market
    All on a market day,
And she fell asleep
    On the King's highway.

There came by a pedlar
    His name was Stout,
He cut her petticoats
    All round about;
He cut her petticoats
    Up to her knees,
Which made the poor woman
    To shiver and sneeze.

When the little woman
    Began to awake,
She began to shiver,
    And she began to shake;
She began to shake,
    And she began to cry,
Goodness mercy on me,
    This is none of I!

If it be not I,
    As I suppose it be,
I have a little dog at home,
    And he knows me;
If it be I,
    He'll wag his little tail,
And if it be not I,
    He'll loudly bark and wail.

Home went the little woman,
    All in the dark,
Up jumped the little dog,
    And he began to bark.
He began to bark,
    And she began to cry,
Goodness mercy on me,
    I see I be not I!

This poor little woman
    Passed the night on a stile,
She shivered with cold,
    And she trembled the while;
She slept not a wink
    But was all night awake,
And was heartily glad
    When morning did break.

There came by the pedlar
    Returning from town,
She asked him for something
    To match her short gown,
The sly pedlar rogue
    Showed the piece he purloined,
Said he to the woman,
    It will do nicely joined.

She pinned on the piece,
    And exclaimed, What a match!
I am lucky indeed
    Such a bargain to catch.
The dog wagged his tail,
    And she began to cry,
Goodness mercy on me,
    I've discovered it be I!

Once I saw a little bird
    Come hop, hop, hop;
So I cried, "Little bird,
    Will you stop, stop, stop?"

And was going to the window
    To say, "How do you do?"
But he shook his little tail,
    And far away he flew.

I had two pigeons bright and gay,
They flew from me the other day;
What was the reason they did go?
I cannot tell for I do not know.

Mary had a pretty bird,
    Feathers bright and yellow,
Slender legs—upon my word
    He was a pretty fellow!

The sweetest note he always sung,
    Which much delighted Mary.
She often, where the cage was hung,
    Sat hearing her canary.

See a pin and pick it up,
All the day you'll have good luck.
See a pin and let it lay,
Bad luck you'll have all the day.

Tickly, tickly, on your knee,
If you laugh you don't love me.

The cock crows in the morn
To tell us to rise,
And he that lies late
Will never be wise:
For early to bed,
And early to rise,
Is the way to be healthy
And wealthy and wise.

Sukey, you shall be my wife
    And I will tell you why:
I have got a little pig,
    And you have got a sty;
I have got a dun cow,
    And you can make good cheese;
Sukey, will you marry me?
    Say Yes, if you please.

The old woman must stand
    At the tub, tub, tub,
The dirty clothes
    To rub, rub, rub;
But when they are clean,
    And fit to be seen,
She'll dress like a lady,
    And dance on the green.

Sing, sing,
    What shall I sing?
The cat's run away
    With the pudding string!

Do, do,
    What shall I do?
The cat's run away
    With the pudding too!

Little Blue Ben, who lives in the glen,
Keeps a blue cat and one blue hen,
Which lays of blue eggs a score and ten;
Where shall I find the little Blue Ben?

Little Nancy Etticoat,
With a white petticoat,
And a red nose;
She has no feet or hands,
The longer she stands
The shorter she grows.

Matthew, Mark, Luke, and John,
Hold my horse till I leap on,
Hold him steady, hold him sure,
And I'll get over the misty moor.

Sally go round the sun,
Sally go round the moon,
Sally go round the chimney-pots
On a Saturday afternoon.

There were three jovial Welshmen,
  As I have heard men say,
And they would go a-hunting
  Upon St. David's Day.

All the day they hunted
  And nothing could they find,
But a ship a-sailing,
  A-sailing with the wind.

One said it was a ship,
  The other he said, Nay;
The third said it was a house,
  With the chimney blown away.

And all the night they hunted
  And nothing could they find,
But the moon a-gliding,
  A-gliding with the wind.

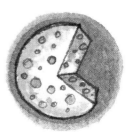

One said it was the moon,
  The other he said, Nay;
The third said it was a cheese,
  And half of it cut away.

And all the day they hunted
    And nothing could they find,
But a hedgehog in a bramble bush,
    And that they left behind.

The first said it was a hedgehog,
    The second he said, Nay;
The third said it was a pincushion,
    And the pins stuck in wrong way.

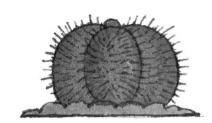

And all the night they hunted
    And nothing could they find,
But a hare in a turnip field,
    And that they left behind.

The first said it was a hare,
    The second he said, Nay;
The third said it was a calf,
    And the cow had run away.

And all the day they hunted
    And nothing could they find,
But an owl in a holly tree,
    And that they left behind.

One said it was an owl,
    The other he said, Nay;
The third said 'twas an old man,
    And his beard growing grey.

Dear, dear! what can the matter be?
Two old women go up in an apple tree;
One came down, and the other stayed till Saturday.

Ding, dong, bell,
Pussy's in the well.
Who put her in?
Little Johnny Green.
Who pulled her out?
Little Tommy Stout.
What a naughty boy was that
To try to drown poor pussy cat,
Who never did him any harm,
And killed the mice in his father's barn.

Ride away, ride away,
   Johnny shall ride,
He shall have a pussy cat
   Tied to one side;
He shall have a little dog
   Tied to the other,
And Johnny shall ride
   To see his grandmother.

Three little ghostesses,
Sitting on postesses,
Eating buttered toastesses,
Greasing their fistesses,
Up to their wristesses,
Oh, what beastesses
To make such feastesses!

Christmas comes but once a year,
And when it comes it brings good cheer,
A pocket full of money, and a cellar full of beer.

God bless the master of this house,
    And its good mistress too,
And all the little children
    That round the table go;
And all your kin and kinsmen,
    That dwell both far and near;
We wish you a merry Christmas
    And a happy New Year.

Christmas is coming,
    The geese are getting fat,
Please to put a penny
    In the old man's hat.
If you haven't got a penny,
    A ha'penny will do;
If you haven't got a ha'penny,
    Then God bless you!

As I sat on a sunny bank
On Christmas day in the morning,
I saw three ships come sailing by
On Christmas day in the morning.
And who do you think were in those ships
But Joseph and his fair lady;
He did whistle and she did sing,
And all the bells on earth did ring
For joy our Savior he was born
On Christmas day in the morning.

Hush-a-bye, baby, on the tree top,
When the wind blows the cradle will rock;
When the bough breaks the cradle will fall,
Down will come baby, cradle, and all.

When little Fred went to bed,
   He always said his prayers;
He kissed mamma, and then papa,
   And straightway went upstairs.

The Man in the Moon looked out of the moon,
Looked out of the moon and said,
"'Tis time for all children on the earth
To think about getting to bed!"

Wee Willie Winkie runs through the town,
Upstairs and downstairs in his night-gown,
Rapping at the window, crying through the lock,
Are the children all in bed, for now it's eight o'clock?

Boys and girls come out to play,
The moon doth shine as bright as day.
Leave your supper and leave your sleep,
And join your playfellows in the street.
Come with a whoop and come with a call,
Come with a good will or not at all.
Up the ladder and down the wall,
A half-penny loaf will serve us all;
You find milk, and I'll find flour,
And we'll have a pudding in half an hour.

The moon shines bright,
The stars give light,
And little Nanny Button-cap
Will come tomorrow night.

Rock-a-bye, baby,
    Thy cradle is green,
Father's a nobleman,
    Mother's a queen;
And Betty's a lady,
    And wears a gold ring;
And Johnny's a drummer,
    And drums for the king.

I see the moon,
    And the moon sees me;
God bless the moon,
    And God bless me.

Star light, star bright,
First star I see tonight,
I wish I may, I wish I might,
Have the wish I wish tonight.

Twinkle, twinkle, little star,
How I wonder what you are!
Up above the world so high,
Like a diamond in the sky.

Sleep, baby, sleep,
Our cottage vale is deep:
The little lamb is on the green,
With woolly fleece so soft and clean—
Sleep, baby, sleep.

Sleep, baby, sleep,
Down where the woodbines creep;
Be always like the lamb so mild,
A kind, and sweet, and gentle child.
Sleep, baby, sleep.

Matthew, Mark, Luke, and John,
Bless the bed that I lie on.
    Four corners to my bed,
    Four angels round my head;
    One to watch and one to pray
    And two to bear my soul away.

Now I lay me down to sleep,
I pray the Lord my soul to keep;
And if I die before I wake,
I pray the Lord my soul to take.

INDEX OF FIRST LINES